For my wonderful friend Judy, who makes
every Hanukkah even brighter—J.S.

For my beautiful daughter Alice—A.R.

KAR-BEN PUBLISHING, INC.
A division of Lerner Publishing Group, Inc.
241 First Avenue North
Minneapolis, MN 55401 U.S.A.
1-800-4-KARBEN

Website address: www.karben.com

Library of Congress Cataloging-in-Publication Data

Sutton, Jane.
  Esther's Hanukkah disaster / by Jane Sutton ; illustrated by Andy Rowland.
    p. cm.
  Summary: "A gorilla named Esther tries—at first unsuccessfully—to give perfect
Hanukkah gifts to all her friends."—Provided by publisher.
  ISBN: 978-0-7613-9043-5 (lib. bdg : alk. paper)
  ISBN: 978-1-4677-1638-3 (eBook)
  [1. Hanukkah—Fiction. 2. Gifts—Fiction. 3. Friendship—Fiction. 4. Jews—
Fiction.] I. Rowland, Andrew, 1962– ill. II. Title.
PZ7.S96824Est 2013
[E]—dc23   2012029131

Manufactured in the United States of America
1 – CG – 7/15/13

ESTHER'S HANUKKAH DISASTER

by Jane Sutton   Illustrated by Andy Rowland

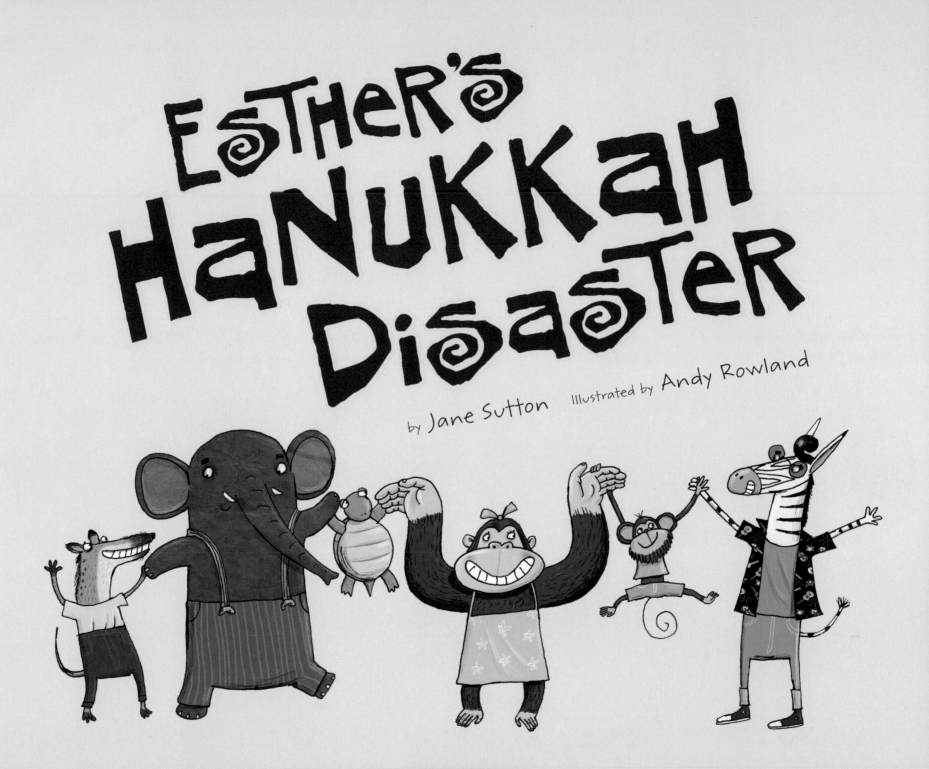

KAR-BEN
PUBLISHING

"Oh dear," Esther exclaimed looking at her calendar. "Hanukkah starts tomorrow night, and I haven't bought a single present for any of my friends!"

Esther ate a big breakfast to give herself strength for a long day of shopping.

When she got to the Jungle Store, she headed straight for the clothing department.

"What unusual socks!" thought Esther.
"I'll buy two pairs for my friend Sarah."

Then she spotted a bright red turtleneck. "I'll surprise my friend Zack with this," she decided.

A sign in the sports department caught Esther's eye. It said: "Jogging Suits on Sale! Marked Down from $13.00 to only $12.99."

"A jogging suit will be perfect for my friend Josephine!" she exclaimed.

Then, Esther was excited to find a jungle gym kit. The box said: "Build your own jungle gym in just 10 minutes...or 10 days at the most!" She grabbed one for her friend Hal.

In the book department, Esther picked up a paperback called *100 Jokes About Elephants*. Joke #52 struck her so funny that she fell down laughing, so she bought it for her friend Oscar.

Then she went home to wrap her gifts.

The next night after the sun went down, Esther placed two candles in her menorah. She lit the shamash candle and said the special blessing. Then she lit the candle for the first night of Hanukkah and said the other two blessings. She remembered the story of the Maccabees and the little jug of oil that lasted eight days.

When the candles had burned down, it was time for Esther to deliver her presents. She loaded them into a wheelbarrow and headed down the road.

Her first stop was Sarah's house. Esther gave Sarah the two pairs of socks. She was sure her friend would admire their unusual design.

"Thank you," said Sarah. Then she burst out laughing and said, "These socks are big enough for an elephant!"

"Oops," said Esther. "I forgot to check the size."

"Don't worry," said Sarah. "Presents are not the most important part of Hanukkah."

Then Sarah handed Esther her present—a bottle of Gorilla-Vanilla perfume.

"Mmm," said Esther, dabbing behind her ears. "Now I smell wonderful!"

Next Esther hurried to Zack's.

When Zack saw the turtleneck, he frowned, "Thank you, Esther, but I never, ever wear red clothing. It's because of that terrible riddle."

"What riddle?" asked Esther.

"What's black and white and red all over?" Zack said with a sigh.

"I don't know...what?" asked Esther.

"An embarrassed zebra," muttered Zack.

Esther roared with laughter. "Oh, I'm so sorry...I can see why you wouldn't ever wear red."

"It's OK," said Zack. Then he gave Esther a year's membership in the Coconut of the Month Club.

"What a yummy present!" said Esther. "Thank you!"

As Esther left Zack's, she thought, "My Hanukkah presents are turning into a disaster!"

Then she went to see Josephine, who had just finished lighting her menorah.

Esther gave Josephine the jogging suit.

"Thanks, Esther dear, but I can't jog!" Josephine giggled. "I'm lucky if I can keep up a fast crawl."

"I forgot," said Esther sadly.

"Not a problem," Josephine said. "Presents schmesents!" But Josephine had a special present for Esther: a costume of a human. Esther had always wanted to dress up as a human!

On the way to Oscar's, Esther rolled her wheelbarrow more slowly. "All my gifts have been dreadful so far," she thought. "Surely Oscar will like *100 Jokes About Elephants!*"

But Oscar told her gently that he thought the book was in very poor taste. "There should be a law against elephant jokes," he said.

Esther wasn't laughing anymore. In fact, she felt more like crying. "I'm sorry I hurt your feelings," she said.

"I know you didn't mean to," he said. Then he gave Esther a book that was perfect for her: *1001 Ways to Serve Bananas*.

Esther's final stop was at Hal's cave. She had been so excited about the easy-to-put-together jungle gym kit. Now she was sure that something would be wrong with it, too. But what?

She soon found out. "Hyenas can't climb jungle gyms like monkeys can," Hal told her.

"Why didn't I think of that?" said Esther.

Hal handed Esther an envelope with two tickets to The Gorilla Theatre.

"Happy Hanukkah!" Hal called to Esther as she was leaving.

But Esther didn't *feel* happy. "No one liked my presents," she thought as she trudged home. Looking at all the fabulous Hanukkah gifts from her friends made her even more miserable.

When Esther got back home, she made herself a cup of tea. Suddenly she had an idea. After all, Hanukkah wasn't over yet. She took out note paper and wrote invitations to her friends: "Please come to my house on the Eighth Night of Hanukkah. Make sure to bring the gift I gave you!"

On the last night of Hanukkah, Esther and her friends gathered around her menorah. She lit the shamash candle and said the blessings. Her friends took turns lighting the other eight candles.

As they watched the candles burning, they sang Hanukkah songs and ate latkes and applesauce.

"What a lovely party, Esther!" said Josephine.

"And the *latkes* were scrumptious!" said Oscar.

"But why did you ask us to bring the presents you gave us?" asked Zack.

"I almost forgot!" she said. "I know that my gifts to you were a total disaster, but now you can trade!"

Esther turned to Sarah. "The two pairs of socks I bought you would fit an elephant," she said. Sarah smiled and handed the socks to Oscar.

Then Esther called on Hal. "Remember when I gave you the jungle gym kit, and you said you weren't a monkey?"

"How could I forget?" said Hal, handing the kit to Sarah.

Zack was delighted to take the jogging suit from Josephine. "Thank goodness it's not red."

When Hal started reading *100 Jokes About Elephants* he began laughing like a hyena, which, of course, he was.

Finally, Zack gave Josephine the turtleneck, and Esther and Oscar helped her pull it over her shell. It fit perfectly.

When her guests had left, Esther smiled to herself.
Her choice of presents hadn't been a disaster after all.

They had brought her friends together, and Hanukkah
had been a great success.

ABOUT HANUKKAH

Hanukkah is an eight-day Festival of Lights that celebrates the victory of the Maccabees over the mighty armies of Syrian King Antiochus. According to legend, when the Maccabees came to restore the Holy Temple in Jerusalem, they found one jug of pure oil, enough to keep the menorah lit for just one day. But a miracle happened, and the oil burned for eight days. On each night of the holiday, we add an additional candle to the menorah, exchange gifts, play the game of dreidel, and eat foods fried in oil—latkes (potato pancakes) and sufganiyot (jelly donuts)—to remember this victory for religious freedom.

ABOUT THE AUTHOR

Jane Sutton grew up in Roslyn, Long Island, where she began writing stories and poems at a young age. She graduated from Brandeis University with a B.A. in Comparative Literature. In addition to writing books, Jane is a writing tutor and teaches a community education class for adults about how to write for kids. She, her husband, and grown children live in the Boston area.

ABOUT THE ILLUSTRATOR

To make the rainy days pass as a child in northern England, Andy Rowland used to draw matchstick men and matchstick cats and dogs on the walls of a coal shed with a piece of coal. Thus began his interest in art. While studying for a degree in Manchester, he accepted his first drawing award, the MacMillan Children's Book Prize. Years later, with over 20 published books under his belt, he has his own coal shed. He still lives in the rainy north of England.

By the way, here's joke #52 in *100 Jokes About Elephants:*

How do elephants talk to each other when they're far away?

On the elephone.